The
Mighty Mastiff
of the
Mayflower

Peter Arenstam

Illustrations by Karen Busch Holman

THE
History
PRESS

Published by The History Press
Charleston, SC 29403
www.historypress.net

Text copyright © 2012 by Peter Arenstam
Illustrations copyright © 2012 by Karen Busch Holman
All rights reserved

First published 2012
Second printing 2013

Manufactured in the United States

ISBN 978.1.60949.609.8

Library of Congress CIP data applied for.

For Sue,
with whom I have shared
a lifelong voyage of discovery.

Contents

The Mayflower

ATLANTIC OCEAN

Plymouth

CAPE COD

CHAPTER ONE

Nearly Over Before It Begins

It is late in the day, late in the year and it may be too late to turn back to land. A mastiff stands on the deck of a small merchant ship named *Speedwell*. Despite her size and the many passengers aboard, she feels small and lonely looking out over the sea. A second merchant ship sailing in company coasts alongside, spilling the wind out of its sails, interrupting her thoughts of home and family. Keeping away a safe distance, the towering ship wallows in the deep swell, exposing its white painted hull with each roll.

"We cannot gain on the leak. I fear we must bear up or sink at sea!" Master Reynolds shouts from the *Speedwell* across the heaving waves. Water spurts from a log pump on deck, worked continuously by two straining crewmen. He raises his voice to be heard over the canvas sails shaking in the steady wind.

"We can scarce free her of water with continued pumping," Reynolds adds. Passengers and sailors line the rails of both ships looking across at one another. The dog braces her paws against the rolling motion, eyeing the distance between the two ships.

"Steady, now. No escaping for you," John Goodman says. He puts his hand on the dog's neck and rubs her fur with affection. "Our lot is here on the *Speedwell*. God will watch over us." The ridges that appear on the dog's forehead suggest she is not so sure.

Looking out at the assembled passengers, the mastiff watches as the deacon staggers to the rail while his young servant Will Butten struggles to support him. The deacon is once again sick into the sea. The rail seems closer to the water's surface than ever before.

"We must bear up and back to land," Reynolds hollers over to Master Jones, standing on the deck of the *Mayflower*. "Or we will all soon be meat for the fishes." They cannot make out Jones's growled reply, but his command to brace around and haul in the sheets for a course to Lands End might have been heard all the way back at Southampton and the pups the mastiff has left behind.

The larger ship surges ahead with the wind in her six sails. The dog on the *Speedwell* watches its stern slide by, the crisply painted carving of a mayflower glowing as it catches the last light of the dying day.

The *Speedwell*, under reduced sail to ease the pressure on the leaking hull, follows the *Mayflower* toward a safe anchorage in the southwest of England. The two days back to land are among the quietest and saddest since the *Speedwell* left Holland in July. The mastiff spends her time on deck dozing in a corner by the forecastle out of the wind and the sailors' way. Her thoughts return to home and her four little ones left behind. She can only guess how they are faring without her.

This is the second attempt to leave the coast of England, and it has ended the same as the first. The leaking *Speedwell* forced both ships to turn back, the first time into Dartmouth. For the mastiff in the pre-dawn light, sniffing the wind at the rail for familiar scents, there is some hope of getting free. Maybe the ship will go all the way back to Southampton this time.

Land looms on the horizon, a dark lump like a sailor's thrum cap, against a backdrop of purple in the sky hinting at where the sun will soon rise. The mastiff focuses on the mass of land as it grows bigger. Everything she knows—her old master, her new litter of pups, the old snug bed and the open fields she used to romp in—is together on the growing bit of home. Her legs tense with the thought of returning, with the hope of springing ashore, with the need to be with her family and care for them, to care for someone.

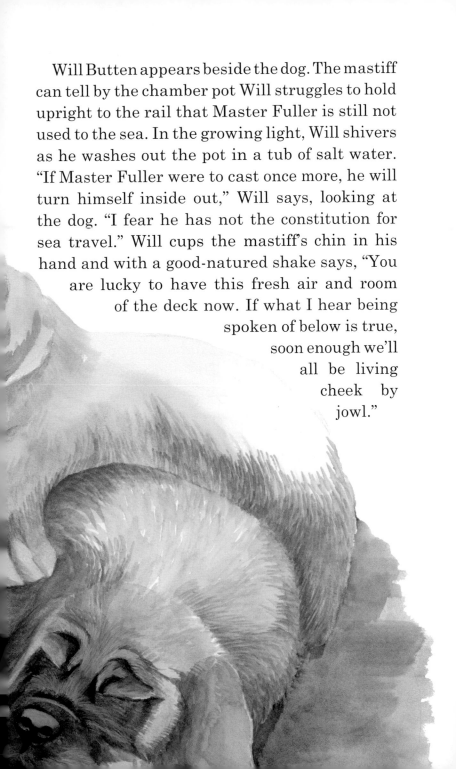

Will Butten appears beside the dog. The mastiff can tell by the chamber pot Will struggles to hold upright to the rail that Master Fuller is still not used to the sea. In the growing light, Will shivers as he washes out the pot in a tub of salt water. "If Master Fuller were to cast once more, he will turn himself inside out," Will says, looking at the dog. "I fear he has not the constitution for sea travel." Will cups the mastiff's chin in his hand and with a good-natured shake says, "You are lucky to have this fresh air and room of the deck now. If what I hear being spoken of below is true, soon enough we'll all be living cheek by jowl."

As the sun rises, the mastiff can make out more details of her surroundings. The English Channel stretches before the ship like the great road to London. Vessels bound on matters great and small make their own way across the waters. Billowing sails dot the scene like white caps at sea. Ahead, the *Mayflower* alters course, veering off for the high hills surrounding the entrance to a great harbor. The mastiff can see it is not Southampton after all. This is not her home.

"Stand by to alter course!" Master Reynolds shouts from his place of command on the deck. "Get the anchors ready to fall," the mate barks at the crew. "We will be anchored off the barbican by six bells." The mastiff turns from the rail. Since they are returning to Plymouth in England and not her home of Southampton, she won't be seeing her family. She has no interest in what is ahead on shore.

CHAPTER TWO

A Last Chance and a New Start

While the crew is busy once again searching out the source of the leak, a small number of passengers on either ship are allowed on shore. The mastiff, happy to have dry land under her paws, even after such a short time at sea, noses about the stack of barrels and chests removed from the *Speedwell* during the repairs. A red spotted spaniel races by, chasing the ship's cat through the maze of provisions.

"Here now," John Goodman shouts. "Come back at once!" He stomps his foot, but the spaniel pays him no mind. "We will not be allowed ashore again if you cannot behave," he calls out to the dog as it disappears. The mastiff has little interest in the chase but watches as the cat streaks up onto a stack of tun barrels,

where she sits smiling down at the two dogs. The mastiff continues her investigation, wandering up the pier, keeping an eye on her new master, John Goodman. The young spaniel runs in circles barking, trying to look menacing, oblivious to everyone.

"You will have to teach those animals to mind," a young man says, walking up to John Goodman. "Or at least recognize when chasing cats is futile. That dog will get in a world of trouble if he remains so undisciplined when we settle in our plantation."

"Aye, the spaniel is a bit boisterous I admit, he is still young after all," Goodman says. "He will settle down in time. It is the mastiff I worry about. She has been calm to the point of sadness. One look into those brown eyes tells her emotions. Ever since Robert Cushman purchased her for us in Southampton, I have been charged with watching over her. She behaves, for all the world, as if she is just looking for a chance to bolt home. Are you part of our congregation?"

"I am Peter Brown, lately of London, now aboard *Mayflower*," Brown says, giving the slightest of bows as he raises his hat just off his head. "No, I am not of your church but will make a new start of it with your company when we land at the Hudson River."

"God grant that it will be so," John Goodman replies.

"God willing and seaworthy vessels," Brown adds, nodding toward the *Speedwell*. The two men look up as Robert Cushman leads the mastiff by her collar back toward the ships. Another, older man follows behind. Everyone on the pier can hear their conversation as they approach.

"It cannot be helped, Master Martin," Robert Cushman is saying. "I have told you many times before. Master Reynolds and the *Speedwell* came highly recommended to us in Holland."

"John Goodman, you must mind our dog for us," Cushman says. "I found her up among the shops in the barbican. If we lose her, there are no spare funds to purchase another. Isn't that right, Martin?" This he says as he turns the mastiff back over to John Goodman. The mastiff huffs and sits down where the men stand. She knows this conversation could go on for some time. These people, she is finding, could spend a day discussing what to have for breakfast.

"We would have spare funds if we didn't have to pay to have your *Speedwell* repaired, twice," Martin says.

"Aye, we might have more funds if you would explain your accounts and the £700 you spent in Southampton," Cushman replies. Martin stands still looking down at the younger Cushman as if he were not good enough to wipe his shoes.

He says in a slow, deep voice, "It is through your poor management of this enterprise that we are short of funds and now own a vessel with water pouring in as if at a mole hole. If we are to get away this year, indeed if this enterprise is to succeed at all, you must arrange to sell off some of that excess butter you purchased. Pay your bills in this port, choose who will go aboard the other ship, who must stay behind with your ill-named *Speedwell* and get this enterprise underway." He turns on his heel and heads for the larger ship tied to the pier ahead of the *Speedwell*. Over his shoulder he shouts, "And, John Goodman, see to it that the mastiff does not wander off again, if you want to stay in my good graces. We can ill afford the time to look for her."

The mastiff perks up her ears at this. The *Speedwell* is to stay behind? If that is so, maybe she can stay with that ship instead of transferring to the larger *Mayflower*. And if the *Speedwell* were to stay in England, maybe she can find a way back to Southampton and her own young pups.

John tugs on her leash. "Come, girl," he says. "I will call you Grace, to remind me how we should all behave," he decides, looking at Martin as he stomps away. The mastiff reluctantly gets to her feet. Peter Brown takes charge of the spaniel and the two men head back to the pier.

"Those two men will not last on the same ship," Brown says, gesturing at Martin and Cushman. "No matter how speedy a voyage we make. There is no room for two men of such hot temper."

"Come, Grace," John Goodman says, coaxing the dog forward. "Fear not, you and I are destined for America. We shall find room aboard *Mayflower*."

With her tail low and her heart heavy, the mastiff walks behind John and Peter to a knot of passengers actively discussing who will continue on and who should stay behind. Time is short and the season is late. Decisions have to be made while the weather still allows them to get away. The mastiff can see that her last chance to break away and head home is upon her.

CHAPTER THREE

And They Were All Compact Together in One Ship

Breaking away is proving harder than it seemed at first for Grace. Despite being busy first packing up his few belongings on the *Speedwell* and then finding a spot to settle in on the ever more crowded *Mayflower*, John Goodman keeps a close eye and a tight leash on the dogs.

The waterfront is alive with activity. The crew is stacking barrels while passengers create a pyramid of chests and pile up mounds of crates. The *Mayflower* sits lower and lower in the water as the sailors wedge the passengers' belongings and supplies for the colony into an ever more tightly packed hold.

Grace sits on the deck of the *Mayflower*, craning her neck while watching the sailors

swarm over the ship's rigging. There are thousands of details, large and small, crying out for attention. Passengers hurry by the preoccupied dog, off to discuss matters of the colony among themselves and to offer advice to a tolerant ship's master.

The sounds of a farmyard bring Grace's attention to a commotion on the pier. Robert Cushman is directing the young servant Will Butten and another young passenger. The boys are doing their best to corral a small flock of goats while they carry a basket containing chickens in each hand. A small cluster of hogs, delivered in a cart earlier, stand surrounded by some hurdle fencing.

"Mind that kid, William," Cushman shouts as a young goat makes a dash away from the flock. Will waves one of the baskets at the goat, and it veers back to its mother's side. On the other side, the boy runs forward as the flock accepts the kid and sways his way. "Steady on there. Lead them to the hog pen." More people drop what they are doing and run down the gangway to assist the young boys.

Grace is alone on the deck for the first time in days. She peers back toward Master Jones's closed cabin door. The passenger leaders must still be inside discussing their departure. She can hear John Goodman down below. He is deep in a conversation about hunting, again, with his new friend Peter Brown. The sailors ignore anything happening below them on the deck as they work away in the rigging. The mastiff pads toward the gangway. This may be the moment she has been waiting for.

On the pier, Robert Cushman continues to shout at the two boys. "No, no, not that way, William! Keep the goats together. Now mind that hog. He will snap at you through the hurdle if you don't have a care."

Grace keeps her head down, imagining it will help hide her as she creeps off the gangway. She puts her paws on the pier. She can see several passengers rushing up with some hurdle fencing to collect the goats the boys are bringing to the ship. If they all just stay busy with the animals for a few more minutes, Grace knows she can make good her escape. Then all she has to do is find her way back to Southampton and her pups.

"There now," Cushman shouts. "You men bring the fencing this way. Steady on. Mind the hogs. I have warned you."

Grace slowly slinks off the pier. The stack of barrels obscures her from the busy crowd. She decides now is the time. She leaps forward, breaking into a loping run. She heads up the hill toward the town and the crowded streets in which she can hide.

Back at the ship, she hears a piercing squeal followed by shouts of surprise and dismay from the crowd. "Ayee, that hog has bit me!" Will exclaims. Grace keeps running up the hill.

"Come back!" she hears Robert Cushman yell. Just then an escaped hog passes Grace, grunting and running up the hill. Young Will Butten follows closely behind, chasing the hog.

The hog and the boy disappear around a corner. The dog ignores them both and runs on. She turns the same corner and runs past an alley in the barbican. She comes to a stop, panting. Turning back, she looks down the length of the alley. William Butten stands at the end, trapped

with his back against a stone wall. He faces an angry hog. Grace can hear John Goodman and Robert Cushman shouting as they run up the hill. She knows she should keep going.

Grace looks again at the frightened boy facing the hog on his own. She gives a deep growl and then a series of sharp barks as she lunges into the alley. The hog turns to face the dog. Will takes the chance to run out of the alley. The dog and the hog circle, sizing up each other, each making a testing lunge at the other.

"Pray, stand aside," Robert Cushman shouts at the mastiff as he wades into the alley between the growling animals. "Don't harm the hog. We need him for breed stock." Robert Cushman swats the dog, and the hog for good measure, as John Goodman comes up with the mastiff's lead.

"That's quite enough, Robert," Goodman says. "There's my girl," he says, hugging the mastiff. "Looks to me like you ran off to save young Butten." Standing up, he slips the lead onto Grace's collar. "There's a good dog." He rubs her face and leads Grace back out of the alley. "Come now, girl, 'tis back to the ship for us. Come, Will, no more playing with the hogs for you my lad. Master Fuller will need you on the ship. We sail in the morning."

Grace stiffens at John Goodman's words and then feels Will Butten's hand rest on her head.

The two look at each other. He gives her a soft pat. The mastiff can see this young boy will need someone to look out for him on the long voyage to come.

CHAPTER FOUR

With a Prosperous Wind and a Diverse Company

For the third time in as many months, Grace is aboard a ship headed to sea. There is the now familiar rush of activity to get the ship out of the harbor. The master, his voice booming out across the decks, directs sailors to weigh anchor. One after another, each sail is set, and the helmsman steers a course for the open sea. The *Mayflower* slowly gathers speed under a great canvas cloud. Near shore, two fishermen stand in a small shallop, hauling their net full of fish, oblivious to the great ship headed out across the Atlantic Ocean.

Grace finds herself at the rail in the crowd of passengers who have come on deck for a final glimpse of England. Most know this is the last they will ever see of their home country. Like the others, Grace is full of a mixture of excitement, sadness and nervousness about the voyage to come. She cannot look back but must gaze ahead to what is waiting for her on the other side of the ocean. From her spot near the rail, she can make out Will Butten supporting Deacon Fuller on the far side of the ship. She makes a move to get to her new friend.

"Martin," the master calls from the half-deck to the governor of the passengers. "Get your people below at once. My men need room to work this ship out of the harbor."

"See here. You all heard Master Jones," Martin says to the passengers around him. "You must clear the decks." No one makes a move to go.

"Robert Cushman is our governor," a Leiden passenger calls out from the crowd. "Cushman is no longer with us. He elected to stay behind. His will may have faltered, but mine has not. For the good of this endeavor and the safety of us all, you must do as directed."

Some of the passengers from London grouse a bit more and suggest they have as much right to be on deck as any other man, but the bosun persuades them otherwise. "Go on now. You heard the master speak. Get yourselves betwixt the decks or I'll start casting you and your belongings overboard." He raises his hand, holding a short length of rope.

There is a bit of shoving. The crowd sways back and forth; the heave of the ship in the swell adds to their movement. Grace can see Will trying to protect Deacon Fuller from the moving crowd. Will topples over, landing on the deacon. Grace puts her head down and tries to plow through the group to get to them.

Other sailors have come to the bosun's rescue. The passengers are quickly divided into two groups. Grace is swept up in the group directed forward to the forecastle ladder that leads below decks. Will and the deacon are flowed into the group that heads aft to the steerage cabin ladder.

"Come, girl, you will need help down the steep ladder," John Goodman says. "I am afraid this ship is not made for passengers like you." Grace takes a last look for her new friend as they head in opposite directions.

"This ship is not made for any passengers," Peter Brown comments. He has helped John Goodman lift the massive dog down to the lower deck. Brown is stooped under the oak beams that support the deck above. This is the first time Grace has been on *Mayflower*'s orlop deck.

"It was through God's providence that this ship was available for hire at all," Goodman says.

"Perhaps it was God's will, and the fact that this ship is past her prime, that we could even afford her at all," Peter Brown says, giving the seemingly stout beam a *thunk* with the side of his fist. A drizzle of dust filters down onto Grace's head, making her sneeze.

"Have a care, my pet," John Goodman says to the dog. "This is too close a space for such outbursts. Come, I have claimed a small space in one of the sections of our own shallop for you and I, and the spaniel, too, if he ever rests."

As if on cue, the spaniel comes racing through the crowded space. He bounces from cabin to cabin, making a circuit of *Mayflower*'s orlop deck, introducing himself to whoever will pat his shaggy head. He noses between two chests to see the Bradfords, William gently talking to his quiet wife, Dorothy. He jumps over some straw bedding to steer clear of the boisterous Myles Standish, explaining in his loud voice tactics of war to his patient wife, Rose. He pauses next to the capstan so the young Brewster boys, Love and Wrestling, can toss him a bit of the ship's biscuit they are eating. The mastiff watches as the spaniel comes skidding to a halt, panting and drooling, bumping into John Goodman, who, with one foot on a gun carriage, is talking earnestly to Peter Brown. The spaniel collapses in a heap next to the mastiff. The great dog acknowledges the spaniel with a sniff but continues to peer into the gloom. Grace tries to see where on the ship the Fuller family has settled with their young servant, William Butten, and how she can connect with him.

CHAPTER FIVE

A Season of Fair Weather and Friendships

It doesn't take long for the entire ship to settle into a routine. Sailors come on deck for their four-hour watch, steering, handling sails or staying ahead of the thousands of ship-keeping demands. All activity is punctuated, every half hour, by the sound of a sailor striking the ship's bell. The bright sun warms the deck and makes the wide expanse of empty sea sparkle. Despite the lateness of the year, the weather remains sweet and fair for a time, so the passengers are allowed up on deck in small groups. The mastiff is in a cluster of people huddled against the cubbridge-head, out of the wind, taking some exercise. At the sound of eight bells, Grace's stomach rumbles. She has already learned it is noon and time for a meal.

The cook appears at the forecastle door. "Where is that yonker of mine? Young, bit of tow, where have you hid yourself this time?" the cook bellows, looking for his assistant. "If you don't show yourself, I'll have every one of those God-fearing passengers in my cook room looking for their meal." This is directed to the ship in general. The passengers understand the message. Their food will be delivered below to them as usual. The cook room is his domain, and no passenger should even think about intruding.

Grace looks up at the foremast over the head of the cook. She watches as two young boys race each other out of the working top and down the backstays. One is Will Butten; the other is the missing cook's assistant, Thomas Carter. Grace heads forward. She has not seen Will since they set out about a week ago. Now here he is dropping down to the deck like a spider from its web. Grace woofs a welcome to young Will, who spots her on the deck. He doesn't see that Thomas has reached the forecastle deck, ready to jump to the cook's aid.

The cook, tired of waiting, is struggling with an iron kettle full of bubbling pottage. "I will tan the back side of that young boy when I see him next," the cook grumbles. "It ain't bad enough I have to feed this crew, but I got to keep alive this lot of pious prayers and money-hunting

grubbers. 'Tis too much to ask for one man." He staggers with the kettle.

Will, looking at the smiling face of the mastiff, is not watching where he lands. Thomas leans over the forecastle head. "Master, pray pardon, Will and I lost track of the hour. I will take that from you," Thomas is saying as Will slides feet first into him so that Thomas pitches over the forecastle deck rail headed for the cook. The mastiff is too late with her warning bark for Will to watch out. Thomas and the cook land in a heap on the main deck. The steaming pottage erupts out of the kettle and coats the pair like well-tarred rigging.

The cook stands up, sputtering and wiping pottage from his face. "It is just as I warned," he is saying to the collection of sailors who have gathered to watch the fun. "These passengers will be nothing but trouble, you mark my words. Did I not say that, bosun?"

Hunger and the desire to help Will get the best of Grace. She takes a great slurp of pottage just as the cook takes a breath to continue his rant. "God's teeth," he roars. "This beast of a dog is attacking me now." He swings at the dog. Will gets himself between the cook and the mastiff and receives the blow intended for the dog. "Have a care, Master," Will says. "This beast, as you call her, is my friend. She wouldn't hurt anyone."

"You best get below where you belong," the cook bellows at Will and the mastiff. "Thomas, come. That was the passengers' meal. The sailors will not go hungry because of this." He collars Thomas and drags him into the cook room, slamming the door behind him.

"I have been looking for you since we left England," Will says as Grace attempts to lick pottage from her jowly face. "I didn't think I would ever find you on such a crowded ship." Will hugs the big dog. Grace nuzzles the boy's knee, leaning into his friend. Her fur flutters in the rising breeze.

"You must get below," says the bosun, who is striding forward along the rail. "All passengers get betwixt the decks. There's a change coming to the weather. We've work to do. "

The mastiff shivers in the rising wind. She hadn't noticed the sun has gone behind a bank of black clouds that blot out the blue sky. "Come with me," Will says to the mastiff. "Now that I have found you, I don't want to lose track of you again." Grace follows Will to the ladder, where she pauses.

"I will help you below," Will says. "We can't let a ladder keep us apart now."

The boy and the dog struggle below to the creaking, rolling orlop deck. It is not necessary to have the mastiff's keen sense of smell to notice the change in the air below decks.

CHAPTER SIX

The Passengers' Will Is Tested

The wind has been howling and the rain pouring down for what must be a week. John Goodman has let Grace stay with the Fuller family and Will Butten in their crowded corner of the orlop deck during most of this time. She is happy watching out for the young servant. Truthfully, there is not much trouble they can get into in such tight quarters.

The same cannot be said for the spaniel. He has visited the mastiff many times in the past few days. The mastiff can tell the young dog is coming her way by the increased shouts and protests as the spaniel bursts over bedding and interrupts dozing and dreaming passengers. He appears with a tangled string from a cat's cradle game hanging from one ear. A collection of young children chase after the spaniel.

"Who's that now? Have a care," Will says. In the dim light, the dog plows into Master Fuller sitting outside his small cabin. "The deacon needs his rest." Grace picks her head up from the beef bone she has been working on. The deck heaves and falls in the great ocean swells. The children come to a halt but pile onto the mastiff. Grace stands up with two of the children still on her back. With a good-natured shrug, she shakes herself free of the laughing children. They land in a heap next to the spaniel. One of the children retrieves her cat's cradle string.

"There you are now, you have your game back. Get yourselves to your families. I am sure they don't want you wandering off, even if there is nowhere to go. This is a ship, not Bartholomew's fair," Will says to the children with a laugh that ends in a cough. The mastiff looks at Will but then notices the spaniel grabbing her beef bone in his teeth and heading up forward toward the goats and hogs. With a concerned look back at Will, she tries to follow the spaniel on the pitching deck. Waves steadily crash into the ship, muffling the noise of disrupted passengers as Grace chases after the spaniel. The ship creaks and moans as it fights with the angry sea.

Grace shakes off the water that is leaking down from the deck above as she tries to catch up with the spaniel. He has dodged in among the goats in their pen in the very forward part of the orlop deck. The ship is rising and falling as it labors to climb over the growing waves. Grace can feel her stomach sway up and down as it follows the motion. She comes to a halt in front of the pen, shakes her head and harrumphs. No one has been able or willing to clean out the pen for some time. The goats are bleating and butting one another, oblivious to everything. They have become used to the wild motion and pungent aroma of their surroundings.

The spaniel is smiling too. He settles next to a prancing goat and begins to gnaw on his captured meal. Grace is about to plunge forward, smell or no, when a terrific boom comes from the middle of the ship. Sounds of splintered wood mix with shouts from sailors and passengers alike. In seconds, tons of water cascade onto the orlop deck. People call out prayers. Master Jones can be heard delivering a steady barrage of commands. The ship slides down a large wave determined to head to the bottom of the sea. Through it all, Grace hears Will's voice among the rest.

She knew she shouldn't have left his side. He needs her now, and she was off chasing that silly spaniel. Looking back through the chaos, she can make out Will trapped under part of the main beam. It has bowed and bent down under the weight of tons of water flinging itself onto the ship. Without further thought, Grace heads for her friend. He is sputtering and coughing and pinned to the deck with a huge splinter of decking through his side.

The sailors and the ship's carpenter are on the orlop deck now. They are focused on the beam and how to keep the ship from sinking. They have no time for Will Butten. Deacon Fuller and the other passengers are still recovering, trying to make sense out of the hole in the

middle of what was once a solid deck and the ceiling of their temporary home.

The mastiff clamps her mouth around the splinter and tugs. Will lets out a scream but immediately feels the relief of the wood removed from his side. He lies back on the deck and lets the water that is washing back and forth rush by and clean the wound. The last he sees, as he closes his eyes, is the mastiff pulling him by an arm away from the wrecked beam and the mass of people hurrying in to save the damaged ship.

Already, the passengers are discussing with Master Jones what should be done. The ship is clearly damaged. They are only halfway across the vast and furious ocean with miles and miles to go, and then what? There are no shipyards to repair the ship, no safe harbors, no support of any kind. A decision to turn back would spell the end of their dream of planting a colony in the New World. Discussion ebbs and flows like the water sloshing across the deck. The mastiff ignores them all. She is doing her best to keep the rolling water from Will. She will not leave his side again.

CHAPTER SEVEN

A New Life and a Death

The mastiff bolts upright, awakened by the sound of Will sneezing and then yelling from the pain in his side. The mastiff shivers and tries to shake the moisture from her damp fur. She watches Will's breath escape from his pinched lips as he grabs his side, closes his eyes again and settles back on his bedding. Families all around quietly huddle in a soggy mass of steaming blankets, trying to take advantage of their collective body heat. Some are praying. All are focused inward on their own thoughts. Waves still bump against the side of the ship but with less fury than before. A sailor, cursing his ill fortune at being on this tempestuous voyage, can be heard throughout the ship.

John Goodman hurries by a cluster of women standing outside two oaken chests topped with bedding, curtained off with scraps of canvas. He nods politely, lifting his hat, but keeps his eyes on the deck. At the Fuller cabin at last, he asks, "How is young Will faring, Master Fuller?" Grace lifts her head upon hearing Goodman's voice. She wags her tail against the damp deck.

"By God's grace and our own mastiff's quick action, the boy will recover, I have no doubt," Fuller replies.

"The dog has already proven her worth to the company," Goodman says. "But, pray, Master Fuller, if she proves a nuisance to you being here, I will take her back with me to my sleeping space."

"I fear she would only find her way back to Will once more," Fuller says. "The two have formed a bond that will not be easy to break in this world, nor would I care to try."

Both men and the mastiff turn their heads in the direction of the curtained-off bedding. They listen as a moan that had been building as the two men talk ends in a sharp cry.

"This is not the first time I have prayed to God that my wife were with us," Fuller says, nodding toward the outburst. "She would be of great comfort to Goodwife Hopkins this day."

"Perhaps the excitement of the storm and our near drowning have drawn out the baby," Goodman replies. The mastiff, remembering her own young ones at home, tries to rise and make her way to the curtained bedding space.

"There now, Grace, even without Mistress Fuller, the Hopkins baby will come without your assistance," Goodman says to the dog. The dog sits again next to Will but continues to watch the curtains behind which Goodwife Hopkins is being tended. Forward of the shrouded bedding, Grace can see boots coming down the ladder from the forecastle.

The ship's surgeon, Giles Heale, is making his way to the orlop deck. The sound of a sailor's cursing follows him below. Giles pauses at the base of the ladder and covers his face in his scarf. "The air grows more thick each time I venture to this deck. How can you abide it?" he says as he approaches Master Fuller. He bends low and removes his cap from his head but continues to hold his scarf over his mouth and nose.

"We have not grown accustomed to the stench, Giles, but we all must abide that which cannot be changed. Surely you are not here to tend the birth of Goodwife Hopkins's child?" Fuller asks. "She has help aplenty for what is now in God's hands." The conversation is punctuated by a cycle of moaning and louder cries, followed by muffled advice from the cluster of women.

"Nay, I have a serious case among one of the crew," Giles says. "I know he has not been the most Christian to your group, but he is still in my charge." The ship heaves and rolls along.

Even the mastiff remembers the sailor. He was always cursing the passengers, laughing at their seasickness, telling them he would make merry with their goods when they perished at sea. The mastiff has taken more than one kick from the bitter man. Now it seems this desperate man is sick and near death himself.

"'Tis the just hand of God," Deacon Fuller suggests. He hands a vial to Giles Heale. "This is a precious mixture for us who are soon to be left in a wilderness, but it may do the poor man some good unless God sees fit to take him." Grace could not see any good from his death either way. It would take every hand aboard this old ship to make it safe to land again.

Giles passes the birthing space on his way to the ladder and the fresh air of the upper decks. The creaking and groaning of the ship, as it works in the sea, competes with the moaning coming from Goodwife Hopkins. The mastiff finds herself drawn to the curtains. The backs of several women can be seen bustling about, the women getting more excited with each passing

moment. The outbursts of Goodwife Hopkins have grown less frequent. There are several moments when no sound comes from within the curtains. The mastiff pushes her head between two unnoticing women. The cry of a newborn babe pierces the silence.

Grace adds her howl of thanksgiving to those being shouted and sung by everyone in the small group. "Oceanus he shall be, then," Hopkins says in answer to a question the mastiff does not hear. The bundle, wrapped in the cleanest sheet they can find, is delivered to Goodwife Hopkins. She holds the baby close to her body for warmth.

The shouting from the upper deck has ceased as well. Giles makes his way down the ladder again. He stands at the bottom, not bothering to hold his scarf up to his face. His face is drawn. "The sailor, the one who was such a bane to you all, is gone. Our fair voyage is now marked by this first death." In his hand he holds a sheet, which will be used to wind the body for its burial into the sea.

CHAPTER EIGHT

And with a Great Seele of the Ship

How Grace might feel about the death of the sailor and the birth of the baby boy, Oceanus, would have to wait. A new storm, one of a series that plagues them across the sea, pounces on the ship with a fury and fierceness as yet unseen on the voyage. For the passengers, the broiling sea and the howling wind just inches from them on the outside of the hull have become so much background noise.

Grace is thankful that Will is up and about again. The wound in his side has ceased bleeding, and he can carefully walk about on the lower deck with only occasional help from the mastiff. He has to stop and lean against Grace when a coughing fit overtakes him. He holds his side with his free hand. The young spaniel spies the pair headed down the deck and overtakes them as Will regains control of his coughing. In the rising storm, objects not tied down begin to slide across the deck.

"You have missed your friend, have you not?" Will manages to get out to the spaniel. The dog bows down and jumps at the older mastiff. Grace shakes her great head, trying to shield Will from the frisky dog. "She has missed you too," Will laughs and bends over, holding his side once more. "Though it may not appear so."

The spaniel, happy for the attention, jumps up and grabs Will's felt hat off his head. The spaniel races away, neatly avoiding a chest as it slides across the narrow pathway. The mastiff harrumphs her displeasure and takes off after

the spaniel, ignoring the chest as it bumps into her side.

The spaniel bounds along with a grin on his face and Will's hat flopping in his mouth. He turns to make sure the mastiff is following. He nips his way forward, bounces over the goat's pen and in one shot is up the ladder to the open deck. Grace skids to a halt at the bottom of the ladder. She has faced this problem before. The ladder is too steep for such a big dog. Will catches up with the mastiff. He leans against the ladder to brace himself against the pitching ship. "You stay here, I will fetch that silly dog. That was my only hat." Will climbs the ladder and disappears into the gloom. The mastiff can hear the roar of waves with the opening of the upper hatch.

Grace watches the goats skitter about on the plunging deck as she waits for Will to return. They stay compact in a small group, laughing in the way young goats will, bouncing off one another and the sow's pen nearby with each surging wave. The sow snorts and grumbles, uncomfortable in the cold damp and unable to free herself from her crate.

The spaniel reappears forward paws first, plunging down the ladder, minus Will's hat. Shaking a torrent of water off his fur, he yips his excitement at his most recent adventure.

He promptly runs to John Goodman and falls asleep between his feet. The mastiff looks from the spaniel up the ladder. Will has not returned. Grace puts a paw on the step of the ladder. It rises up over her head into darkness.

Grace needs to find a way to get up the ladder and on deck. Will is up there and may need her. She tries to throw herself up the ladder in the way the spaniel did but only manages to bump her head and slump down onto the deck in a heap. The goats bound over her as the ship continues to fight against the storm. The sow's crate creaks and groans in the motion. It begins to slide this way and that.

Grace stands up, watching the crate. The goats follow it as it slides farther and farther

with each roll of the ship. The crate stops as the ship settles into a wave trough. As the ship climbs again, the goats get to their feet. They tumble forward. The ship reaches the crest of a wave and plunges down its backside. The goats, down below in one big group, butt into the crate. The sow squeals, the goats bleat and the mastiff yowls as the crate slides once more and bumps into the ladder. Grace sees her chance. She bounds from the deck to the crate and then up the ladder and scrambles outside to the open deck. She finds herself in the midst of a raging storm.

The upper deck is an alien world to the mastiff. Mountains of water roll toward her. Some break in harmless white froth nearby. Others tower over the ship until, with a roar, they cascade down onto the deck, intent on forcing the ship below the surface. The wind shrieks through the rigging. The sailors have lashed down all yards, topmasts and anything that could be lost overboard. Nothing moves on the deck except rivers of water flowing between the frames back over the side to the sea.

Grace sees sailors gathered at one rail. She wonders, only for a moment, what John Howland is doing on the deck in this weather. Their shouts are lost in the chaos of the storm. Something flapping in the air catches her eye. It is Will's hat. He is holding it in the wind, looking out at the monstrous waves. The hat vibrates in the air. Grace barks once, sharp and clear. Will turns and sees her.

"Have you never seen a more awesome sight?" he shouts to the dog. "It is as though we are witnessing the creation. All is turmoil and darkness." The mastiff is uneasy with Will so close to the rail. The ship dips down as a great rolling wave slides under the ship. Will loses his footing. The next wave lands on deck, sweeping everything before it. Water pours over the side. Will looks like he is swimming in a stream. The ship rolls again. Grace can see Will is headed for the rail.

Without a second thought, she lets out a bark and lunges for her friend as the stream of water he is caught in flows back to the sea. She fights against the salt water and grabs Will by his collar just as his feet slip through the rail. Grace braces her paws on the sloping deck. She pushes back. The water slides away, and with a yank, Will is safe on the deck once again.

CHAPTER NINE

Land To!

Weeks have passed since Grace saved Will from sliding off the *Mayflower* mid-ocean. All the talk of the lower deck has revolved around John Howland and how he miraculously saved himself by grabbing a topsail halyard. No one paid any mind to Will Butten and how, if it weren't for the mastiff, he would have slipped off into the sea that very same day.

Grace is not focused on any of the stories being told on the orlop deck just now. She only has time for Will. He has been abed since the storm.

"You are kind to tend me, Master," Will says to Master Fuller.

"It is no more than you had done for me at the start of this voyage," Fuller replies.

"Yet I should be up and caring for you," Will says, trying to rise, the blankets sliding to the deck. He shivers and coughs uncontrollably. The mastiff lifts the blankets off the deck.

"There now," Fuller says, taking the blankets from the dog and pulling them up over Will. "You must rest, Will. Word has gotten around the ship that we are approaching our destination. It will only be a few days until this dreadful voyage has passed. You must save your strength for when we land."

"I am burning up, yet I feel so cold," Will says, shaking as he clutches his bedclothes.

"Come, Grace, lay by Will. He needs your warmth." Fuller pats the bedding next to Will. The mastiff curls up next to the sick boy, laying her head across his legs. Will keeps his hand on her head. The ship sails on with an easy motion that has become all but forgotten by everyone on board. Grace gazes at Will, watching as he shuts his eyes in sleep. There is a sense of stillness on the lower deck as tensions of the long sea voyage seep away.

In the morning, John Goodman comes by the Fuller cabin with Peter Brown to fetch the mastiff. "Come, Grace. We are to be allowed on deck for the morning. We all could use the fresh air." Grace lets herself be coaxed away from the sleeping Will Butten, who has tossed and turned all night but seems to be resting quietly now. Peter Brown and John Goodman push and pull the great dog up the ladder to the main deck.

It is a different world on deck this morning. The full force of the sun shines down on the deck, causing steam to rise up from the soaked wood planks. Sailors have all the sails set. The graceful curves of canvas gather the gentle breeze and pull the ship onward. Groups of passengers stand near the rail, lifting their faces and their tired arms toward the heavens, trying to soak up the warmth of the new day.

The quiet of the morning is interrupted by a cry out of the skies. Everyone on deck turns and looks forward. Grace can see a sharp-winged bird circling over the water ahead. The bird hovers over something floating in the water. A lookout, all the way up on the foretop crosstrees, calls to the deck. "Somfing floating in the water, two points off the starboard bow." The *Mayflower* alters course at the command of Master Jones.

Grace pushes her way through what has become a crowd at the rail. The ship slides along beside the object in the water. Another gull has appeared hovering over the sea. "Do you see it, Grace?" John Goodman calls. Other passengers cry out in recognition. "It comes from our new home. The last storm must have swept it out to sea. We must be close now."

Peter Brown moves aside to make room for the great mastiff. With her paws on the rail, she can see the tree bobbing in the short waves. Gulls are circling over it, dipping down in the disturbed water, trying to catch breakfast. Some passengers pray, some sing and everyone, including the sailors, shouts out with joy. This tree, this floating bit of the land, can only mean one thing. This long, dangerous voyage is near its end. Soon they can all return to their proper element: solid land.

"Governor Martin, you must send all passengers below," Master Jones calls out from the half-deck. "My men must prepare the ship for when we sight land." Grace once again is brought down to the dank orlop deck, leaving the sounds of commands to "ship the anchor hawser" and "prepare the ship's boat to be towed astern." She lets out a massive sneeze as she reaches the bottom of the ladder. The smell of the close quarters is powerful after the free air of the open deck.

In the dim light, Grace tries to reach the Fuller cabin and her friend Will. People everywhere are excitedly chatting and collecting their belongings as if they will step off the ship immediately upon sighting land. Grace can see Master Fuller hunched over outside his cabin. The curtains are pulled shut, and several passengers have gathered around. Giles Heale is speaking to Fuller in a quiet tone.

"It was God's plan for Will," the deacon is saying to the surgeon. "Yet I cannot find the sense in it. He was brave and good and took great care when I was ill."

Grace has a puzzled look on her face. The excitement and happy feelings of just a few moments ago are gone. She cannot bring herself to look inside the cramped cabin. "Ah, there you are," Fuller says to the mastiff. "You were a kind and good friend to Will. His health and wounds were too much for the young boy." Fuller's voice cracks as he hugs the dog. "It was not for him to see the New World." Grace slumps down to the deck. Her one new friend is gone.

She wakes sometime later. It has always been hard to tell what time of day or night it is on the shuttered orlop deck. The Fuller cabin stands open and empty. She lies quietly on the deck, willing the gently rolling deck to lull her back to sleep and dream of her pups and a time before this voyage. A voice reaches down from high in the rigging. All the passengers have heard it and are stirring. Grace lifts her head. The voice calls out again. It is the words so many have waited to hear for over sixty days. It is the sound of a new chance.

"Land, to!"

CHAPTER TEN

First South, Then North and Finally at Anchor

Grace is on deck again with many passengers. The new day and the sight of land growing out of the sea bring an animation to the passengers not seen since Plymouth. The mastiff is a stark contrast to their excitement. She slowly pads up and down in the waist of the ship with her tail low. With the ship's boat off its cradle and being towed behind the *Mayflower*, there is more room on the main deck for the passengers. Sailors peel back layers of canvas off the empty hatch, worn by the pounding sea, allowing much-needed light and air to the orlop deck.

The spaniel, free to roam the open deck, bumps into passengers and sailors alike with his usual high energy. "Take heed," William Bradford says to the dog as it collides with his wife standing next to her husband at the rail. "We are not all ready for such exercise as you." The dog shakes his head and rambles off. Bradford gestures to the land, saying to his wife, Dorothy, "It may look desolate now, my dear, but in time there will be towns with fair houses and grand inns ready to entertain a weary traveler in from a sea of troubles."

Master Jones gives a command, and the ship veers away from the shore as if headed back out to sea. "What is the meaning of this?" Martin shouts to the master of the vessel. "Should we not make all haste to find the mouth of the Hudson River?"

"Martin, this is not the northern parts of the Virginias," Jones says with not a little annoyance in his voice. "We have touched to the north of our intended destination. You are all gazing at Cape Cod, or Cape James, as Captain John Smith did name it. We have some one hundred miles to travel to the south if we are to reach the Hudson. I will not risk my ship so close to shore among the dangers of the shoal water of Tucker's Terrour."

Grace takes little notice of any of this conversation. She has no interest whether they land here or the Hudson River or just sail on forever. Her only friend on the voyage is gone, and she has no energy or ambition to start over again in search of a new charge to look out for and care for.

Throughout the rest of the day, the *Mayflower* ghosts along the shore. The deep scent of soil and wood smoke wafts over the water. Grace sniffs in the scents with a pang of homesickness and longing. The sun, never high in the sky this time of year, starts its descent behind the land. Grace can hear the muffled sound of waves washing over sand. At first, the sound comes from ahead of the ship, but soon they are nearly encircled by white water collapsing in shallow water.

"Prepare to come about!" shouts Master Jones from the half-deck. "The shifting shoals have nearly caught us." The passengers on deck rush to the rail. In the light breeze, their combined weight heels the ship slightly. "We have come so far, God would not let us wreck on the shore," Goodman reasons. The mastiff looks out over the miles of shallow water that stretch away to the south. It is not a fit place for man or dog to step ashore. The *Mayflower* slowly pivots and points back northward. "It is decided," Jones says, gesturing back toward the shoals and addressing the passengers on the main deck. "It will soon be dark. Only a fool would continue south from here. I will not endanger my ship any further. I must still return to England on the *Mayflower* even if you are all bent on staying on this side of the Atlantic." No one argues the point. Passengers, sailors and every animal aboard are heartily weary of the sea.

By morning of the next day, the *Mayflower* rounds the point of the cape and heads in toward shore. Perched out on the side of the ship, a sailor swings the lead line, measuring the depth of the water as the ship eases into the harbor. Grace, like all the passengers and most of the sailors, is paying more attention to the land than what is happening on the ship. She doesn't know what to make of this wild place.

The mastiff slowly spins around in her place on the main deck. The ship is nearly encircled by land. "This cape will provide a secure anchorage," Goodman is saying to Peter Brown.

"Aye, that it will," Brown replies. "But what of the land? Can we plant and grow our crops here? Will there be water at hand?"

"And what of the natives?" Goodman says. "I have heard stories of how fiercely they defend their lands."

"It is certain," Brown replies. "It is well that we have brought our mighty mastiff as guard and companion as we range about this land." Brown rubs Grace's great jowls and shakes her head, coaxing a smile from the downcast dog.

Grace shivers her coat and shakes her head at the human contact. She has kept her distance from the other passengers. If it is her lot to stay in this wild country, she can at least watch out for these two men who seem to care so much for her. Her thoughts are interrupted by a cry from the half-deck.

"Let fall the anchor. Back the fore topsail."

The splash that follows can only be the sound of the anchor leaving the side of the ship and making its way to the harbor mud. The *Mayflower* swings to her anchor and for the first time in sixty-six days, is still.

CHAPTER ELEVEN

Searching for a Settlement

Grace paces the main deck. The ship's boat went ashore with a group of well-armed men almost as soon as the ship's anchor came to rest in the harbor mud. Grace is not eager to get to land. She is not eager to stay aboard. She just pads restlessly up and down the deck, oblivious to the whirlwind of activity. Psalm-singing passengers pile soiled clothing in a heap on the deck. The collective stench rises in visible waves in the weak November sun. Sailors pry up the main hatch boards, eager to air out the ship. Children chase one another along the waist, fearless now on the stationary ship.

"Grace, come," John Goodman calls the mastiff to him. He stands at the boarding ladder at the rail. Grace lifts her head and shambles over to John. He rubs her head with his two hands the way he knows she likes. "It is now your time to aid us in the task for which we have journeyed so far. Master Jones has need of your protection ashore."

"Come, Goodman, the boat has returned. Order the dogs for the exploration parties," Bradford says, looking down at the sad dog. "We must put the voyage in the past. This vast wilderness is now before us. The great mastiff will go with Master Jones. We shall take the spaniel in our party. That is settled."

John Goodman looks again at Grace; her sad eyes look back. She knows they must all do what is necessary. All they have to rely on is one another. She allows herself to be lowered into the boat with Master Jones and some of the leaders of the colony. John Goodman waits on the ship for the next trip ashore.

"I urge you all to make haste," Jones says to Carver as they are rowed ashore. "You must choose a site to make your settlement. I do not wish to linger here long."

Grace looks back at the *Mayflower* swinging to an anchor in the harbor. This ship has been her home now for months. It is the last link with England and her family there. It is where she came to be friends with Will, and soon even the ship will be gone. Grace turns back toward the shore. If she is to survive, she must look forward. Grace knows she will have to learn quickly what it takes to get by in this new land. The ship's boat drifts to a stop in the sand near shore. Without hesitating, she leaps from the boat and splashes into the cold water of the bay. The wet sand slips between her paws as she climbs up the beach. She has arrived at her new home.

Grace is patient with the men as they clamber out of the boat and wade ashore, holding their weapons high out of the salt water. Her legs are none too steady. She has become so used to the motion of the ship that the solid feel of land under her paws makes her knees weak. "God be praised," Carver declares. "At last we are on our proper element once more." The passengers and sailors in the small group kneel or stand as their conscience dictates. "We must all say a prayer of thanksgiving for being delivered into this wild and beautiful new home." Grace sniffs her way up the beach to the crest of the dunes.

Down at the shore, she sees the boat is returning from the *Mayflower* with a second group of passengers. John Goodman and Peter Brown are among them. They are bringing the spaniel with them. The impatient dog doesn't wait; he leaps from the boat before it comes near the shore. The spaniel surfaces with a surprised look on his face, circles the boat once and then swims toward shore. He runs out of the surf and shakes himself off in the midst of the group of men.

"Blast, Goodman," Jones says. "This spaniel could benefit from my bosun's discipline."

"Pray, pardon, Master Jones," Goodman says, tugging at the dog, who continues to smile despite the yanking.

"Come, we will head toward the high ground while you strike out down the beach," Jones says to the groups. "I will take the mastiff. Your group," he says, looking out from under the wide brim of his cap, "can have that spaniel." He whistles for Grace. She trots along, catching up with the well-armed and plodding men.

As they walk along, the joy Grace felt at being on land gives way to

uneasiness about this new world. Some things look familiar to her. The oaks, pines, sweet-smelling juniper, even the holly and walnut trees growing above the beach remind her of home, but there is something different here, something that she has never sensed before.

Ahead, five or six tall men walk out of the forest. Grace immediately notes a dog with them. This new group does not see her or the others from the ship. Her loneliness and her desire to find a new family overcome her caution. She barks a hello at the new dog. She plunges down the hill. Down on the beach, John Goodman's group looks back at the sound of Grace's barking. The native men notice the Englishmen on the shore.

The two groups look at each other for a moment. "Come, Grace!" Goodman shouts as the dog runs after the natives and their dog. The natives turn and run for the cover of the forest ahead. Grace plunges into the trees out of sight. John Goodman and the other men stand looking where Grace has disappeared and then follow at a trot after the great mastiff.

CHAPTER TWELVE

Ancient People in a New World

Grace lunges into the trees. She is determined to catch up to the new dog she saw on the beach. Low branches slap at her face and trace lines along the length of her body. Her chest heaves as she runs. The months of inactivity and small rations of food on the ship have left her weak. She quickly slows and then stops, panting by a creek, too tired to take a drink.

First the spaniel and then John Goodman and the other men catch up with Grace. They gather around her, pivoting their weapons as they try to penetrate the trees with their gaze. "This is not the New Forest of home," Goodman says to the panting dog. "You must stay close at hand. For your protection and ours," he adds, looking up at the men around him. They continue to look cautiously into the trees.

"Aye, just so, Goodman," Standish adds. "Until we see how the natives will receive us, it is best to stick together. That includes the mastiff." The military leader hitches up his breastplate and wipes his brow with the exposed cuff of his sleeve.

"It is no more than we all agreed to in signing the compact," Bradford says, looking back from his position. "Is that not right, Hopkins?" Bradford and Standish look to Stephen Hopkins, who stands off on his own, ignoring the conversation. "Are we not all English men, bound by the rule of English law?"

"Come, it will be dark soon. We should make camp or try to return the ship," Goodman says. "We have discussed this at length even before we landed."

"Just so," Standish agrees, eager to regain control. "Let us make our rendezvous here and see what the new day will bring."

The new day and the many days that follow bring much labor for all and no time for rest or discussions of their legal obligations to one another or the king. There are times of uncertainty, for sure, doubt whether they will ever find a suitable site on which they can settle and concern over the absence of meaningful contact with any native people.

Grace carries on with a heavy heart, but she has little time to think of her losses. She is called upon to go with this group or that, into the forest to where they are cutting juniper branches to burn on the ship or to trudge up and down the beach hunting fowl with the spaniel, John Goodman and his fast friend, Peter Brown. One morning, she situates herself in the shallop as twenty-four men and ten sailors set out in the two small boats from the tip of Cape Cod to continue to look for a settlement site.

The weather is cold and windy. Spray flies off the bows of the boats and freezes on Grace until her fur glistens like leaded glass. She shakes her coat, shattering the ice crystals as the two boats, under the command of Master Jones, head down the bay.

Grace is again called on to walk with the lead group of explorers as they tromp their way over hills, following deer trails through thickets and grassland. Several times she pauses, sniffing on the wind, as they approach silent clearings. The winter wind whips the explorers' cloaks as they stand looking at native houses, trying to determine the last time people lived there.

Grace can sense there is no one about; the site has a feeling of emptiness but not abandonment. The men discover corn buried in woven bags by absent natives for spring planting. There is much debate, after which the men decide to remove some of the corn for their own springtime fields.

They assure each other that they will pay the natives for what they have taken—that is, if they ever come across any on this windswept cape.

That evening, the men build a shelter of tree branches, staking up logs as a means of protection. "Take care, leave no space between those timbers," Standish directs the others. "Our barricade must protect us against the wind as well as native arrows."

"We may not have so much worry of the natives if we had not trespassed on some of their graves, as well as dug up their corn," John Goodman says. "It would be most odious to us if it were our dead they disturbed." Grace shivers at the memory of seeing the graves, encircled like a churchyard in England, one bundle of small bones packed in a fine red powder near other adult-sized bundles.

"Any native we have seen in this place runs at our approach. I would that it were always to be so," Standish says.

"The corn we have taken, placed where God would have us find it, may be the only thing that we will have to sustain us in the coming year," Bradford adds. "Whether the natives object or no."

When the barricade is finished, Grace settles near the fire as some men find places to sleep while others keep guard. The fire snaps and sparks in the quiet of the evening. A blanket of stars blazes overhead.

Toward dawn, one of the men runs into the camp, shouting, "Arm yourselves, there are men, natives about!" Grace bolts up, ready to leap toward the danger. Standish jumps to his feet with his musket. He fires, and other men get off shots. The fur on Grace's neck bristles at the dreadful cry of the natives. She has never heard such a sound before. Arrows *thunk* against the logs of the barricade. The men's muskets crackle in reply. Grace can see the natives steeling for an approach. A large man brandishes his bow. He fires his arrows and stands as the English men fire back.

More men fire their weapons and leap to chase the natives. Grace, among them, runs along the beach. The natives disappear into the trees. "Stand down, men. We have fought them off. Let us not get tangled in their trails," Standish calls to the running men.

They hastily decide to sail on. "While it pleased God to vanquish our enemies and deliver us from this danger, it would seem best if we search for a more hospitable site for our plantation," Bradford suggests. Everyone boards the shallop, Grace taking her place near the bow, and the band of Englishmen moves on from the disturbed lands of Cape Cod.

"I know of a place that may suit you well for your settlement," one of the sailors says. He describes a harbor with fresh water, hills near the shore for a fort and vast lands suitable for farming. He fails to mention that it is known among sailors as Thievish Harbor.

CHAPTER THIRTEEN

From Patuxet to Plimoth

Grace watches the shoreline slide by as the shallop slips up and over each short wave. No one in the boat speaks. They are each in their own world of contemplation. It starts to snow. Grace feels the wet flakes settle on her fur and melt into her skin. She shivers, flapping from ears to tail, to keep warm. Ahead, in the coming darkness, waves crash on a beach.

"Listen to the wind," John Goodman says. "It moans in the boat's rigging like a spirit wandering the world." Several sailors sitting nearby nod, trying to peer into the snow squall. The boat is jumping now.

The mate steering the struggling shallop calls out, "Be of good cheer, all, for I see the entrance to the harbor ahead." It is then that the rudder

breaks and the boat veers around broadside to the waves. "Cast off the sheet," the mate shouts, "spill the wind or we will all perish!" The shallop rolls dangerously from side to side, nearly dipping the rail below the waves. Grace, looking in the direction they were heading, barks sharply. Angry waves batter the shoreline.

"We have run afoul of the shoals. I fear this is not the harbor I took it for," the mate calls out. "Men, we must row ourselves to safety." The sailors fight to use the long sweeps to move the shallop. "Row together lads, or we will certainly die together." The shallop slowly comes back on course as the sailors pull on the sweeps and the sail bulges full of wind. The mast groans with the strain. "I can see calm ahead, for certain," John Goodman calls back to the mate. He stands in the bow next to Grace, who does her best to blink away the whipping snow. As they surf through the breakers into calm water, the strength of the wind is too great for the mast and sail. In three loud cracks, the mast shatters and falls away to leeward. The sailors wrestle with the soaked sail. Grace uses her teeth to help haul the canvas back aboard. The shallop glides to a stop on the back side of a small island out of the wind. In the dark, the mate's call to set an anchor is quickly followed by a splash and then stillness.

They spend the next day on the small island on which they nearly wrecked. In the distance, the mainland curves around them. They are enclosed in a small bay. Looking around at the tree-covered land, Grace sees no telltale smoke of a native cooking fire anywhere. After the Sabbath, also spent on the island, the men venture by shallop to the mainland.

Wary of further damaging the shallop, the mate directs the boat with caution as they approach shore. "Have a care," he calls from his place in the bow. "Sound the lead. This is a shallow harbor. Steer clear of that rock," he says, pointing to a large boulder sitting by itself on the shore. "We must keep this boat in one piece if we are to make it back to the *Mayflower*."

Standing beside him, Grace can see they are maneuvering to head into the mouth of a stream. The steep bank will make getting out of the high-sided boat easier. The shallop slows to a stop in the muddy river bottom. In the silence that follows, Grace again is the first to leap ashore. The riverbank is grass covered, with low bushes growing right up to the water's edge. Grace shoulders her way through the growth.

The first thing Grace notices is the lack of motion. The landscape is still. There is no life here. A dried cornstalk leaf flutters up the open hillside on the breeze. Grace follows it with her eyes. It flattens itself against a native house. The flap of deerskin in the doorway flips and Grace growls quietly in her throat, but no one emerges from the darkened space.

"It would seem God has cleared this land of natives. Yet we must take care," the mate calls to the men who are walking away from the shallop. "We dare not risk another encounter like that on Cape Cod." Grace is now in a far field, sniffing at the base of four poles lashed together with a raised platform above. With her nose, she turns over a red clay pot she finds in a tangle of weeds. Bits of dried food cling to the bottom of the pot. Any scent of the person eating from the dish is long gone.

"Come, Grace," John Goodman's voice echoes down the hillside. He and Peter Brown have climbed to the very top of the hill. Grace tries to picture the people who left all this behind. Where did they go? Have they journeyed far, like she has? But unlike her, they have left behind no one who knows where they went.

"Grace, come," John Goodman shouts. Grace turns away from the pot and empty field. She bounds up the hill. Standing on the crest of the hill, panting from her run, she looks from the land sweeping away from her feet to the water far below. Other men join Goodman and Grace.

"We cannot hope to find better," Goodman says.

"From this hill we can defend our town," Standish says.

"Just so, and there is much fresh water and cleared fields," another man says.

"Ah, but that only means the timber to build our houses must be transported a greater distance," someone else adds.

"We shall lay out the town with a crossroad hard by the brook we have just sailed into," another says.

"Aye, the first street of our new plantation will run down this hill to the water."

"The harbor is secure for certain," the mate adds, "but there is little water at low tide for great ships to enter."

"All the better for our defense," Standish adds. "No foreign ship will be able to enter and fire upon the town of New Plimoth."

Grace listens to the men discuss the good and bad points of settling in the abandoned native town. She can see past the harbor with its small island on one side and the narrow spit of land running out from the other side to Cape Cod Bay. Then there is the vast Atlantic, with her family on the far side. They are so out of her reach they might as well be on the moon she can see rising away to the east out of the sea, cold, distant and silent.

CHAPTER FOURTEEN

A Season of Change

There is little time for reflection or longing during this winter season. The sailors systematically empty the ship of the colonists' goods. Many passengers still live aboard the *Mayflower* but travel by small boat to shore to continue the labor of building a new colony. Some have started to cough and shiver with fever, yet everyone is at work. Men fell trees and saw logs into planks for the first six or seven houses they are building. Women bundle thatch or apply the muddy daub to the walls inside the houses. Grace and the spaniel spend their time with one person or another off hunting food for everyone's meals or just exploring the nearby countryside.

"The sooner we finish a common house, the better," John Goodman says. He and Peter

Brown are walking with two young assistants toward a swath of reeds growing along a narrow creek. The dry grass chatters in the breeze. "Now that illness has taken hold among the people, it is best we get them off the ship and to a secure shelter on land."

"Aye, we have all grown weary of the closeness of the ship," Brown says. "Yet I fear we lack the protection we need on the land." He gestures past the old cornfield they are skirting to the nearby forest. The smoke from several cooking fires hangs in the cold air. "What natives there are here are not eager to show themselves. Yet they are not afraid to make their presence known."

Goodman looks forward to the dogs trotting ahead and then back at the two boys dawdling behind. Grace and the spaniel are eagerly on the trail of another new scent that begs for investigation.

"Come, boys!" Goodman shouts to the boys. "I promised your mothers I would keep my eye to your safety. We must not get separated if we are to make use of this fair day to cut as much thatch for roofs as we can." The two boys, carrying sticks as if they were muskets, stalk along, showing little fear and less understanding of their surroundings.

By midday, the men have cut a wide swath through the dried reeds. The boys have done their best to gather the stalks into armloads they can then bind up as bundles of roof material. The spaniel has spent the morning chasing a chipmunk through the tall grass. After a nap in the January sun, Grace noses along the creek, quietly following the scent of a deer.

"We have earned a rest, have we not?" Goodman calls out to the others. The boys drop the bundles they are working on and immediately fish into the sack of provisions. All four settle into a sunny spot among the reeds to eat and rest. After a while, Goodman and Brown rise. "What say we walk along this creek? We may find a lake that feeds it or some of the natives we have yet to converse with."

Brown stands with his hands on his hips and leans back. "It will do me good to stand upright for some time. Stooping to cut thatch all this morn has bound up my back tight." He gazes about.

"Now where have those dogs gotten off to?" John Goodman gives a piercing whistle, but all is still. The two men set out, following the line of the water up the hillside and toward the forest. The distant sound of barking gives them a direction to start to look. The boys stay behind to finish the work they so hastily dropped for their noon meal.

By the time the sun sets, Grace knows she will be in the woods all night. Chasing after the spaniel who was chasing after the deer she had so patiently stalked all morning had seemed like a good idea, but now that it is getting dark, she is starting to worry. She long ago lost a sense for where she is. Standing still in the gloom, she no longer hears the spaniel baying. Night animals are waking, and she is alone.

Weary and drained, Grace tries to curl up at the base of tree, but the sounds of the dark forest keep her from getting any sleep. She stands listening. She is thirsty and hopes the babble of the creek will come through the still woods. The only sound she hears is the great hoot of an owl. It has found its dinner. Grace shies away, wandering through the trees, feeling more alone than ever before.

Is this to be her lot, Grace thinks to herself, to wander alone and lonely in the great woods, wary of every sight and sound? This is not the life she imagined she would have back before this voyage began. She believed that she would grow old with her family around her, the young pups growing up to have pups of their own. That life had passed her by. She won't have that life. Grace pricks her ears at a distant sound.

It is a wild animal she has never heard before. She starts off in the opposite direction. She hears another sound. The faint cry of a struggle comes to her. Instead of running away, she pauses. Could it be the voices of John Goodman and Peter Brown? Are they in these woods too? She tries to quiet her breath to listen. The wild animal cries again. The men have risked their lives to look for her, she realizes. She can't leave them to fight off the animal alone.

She takes off in the direction of the confrontation. A dusting of snow and dry leaves flies up in her path as she races toward the two men. She weaves around dark tree trunks and over fallen logs. The hooting owl swoops overhead in the other direction. As the sounds of the fight get louder, she slows and creeps along in the underbrush.

She peers through the bushes. It is John Goodman and Peter Brown. The roar sounds again. "It must be the call of a lion, for I know of no other animal that could growl so fiercely," Goodman says. "If it comes near, we must seek safety in the tree." The sound of a twig snapping comes from the direction of the roar. A wildcat walks into view with its mouth open and its tail twitching.

"It will trap us in the tree if we try to climb," Brown says, casting about for some sort of weapon. "I fear it can climb faster than either of us." The cat approaches warily. The two men are unsure what to do.

From behind, they hear something crashing through the branches. As the two men turn to look at the new danger, two branches sweep open and Grace lunges out of the darkness. Her face looks fierce, and her sharp teeth snap. She lands between Goodman and Brown. Goodman grabs hold of her neck and prevents her from following the wildcat, which has turned and disappeared into the forest.

Grace sits panting between the two men. She has survived her night alone in the woods and has even come to the aid of two men who have watched over her since the *Mayflower* voyage began.

CHAPTER FIFTEEN

Mayflower Departs, a New Chapter Begins

It has been a long cold winter for Grace and the remaining passengers from the *Mayflower*. There are far fewer people now than when they first came to New Plimoth in December. The illness and deaths that have swept through the colony have slowed. The early March sun feels warm on Grace's thin body. As she makes her way up the dirt path they call the first street, Grace shakes her fur, loose without a layer of fat to fill out her figure. She is reduced to only that which is necessary for her to survive. Her tail is up, but her head is down.

From the crest of the hill near the gun platform protecting the town, Grace watches two figures approach the settlement. The taller man, Samoset, has been here before, but Grace does not recognize the second man. At a cry from the town, several men hurry up the hillside to greet the newcomer.

"I have brought the last man of Patuxet to you," Samoset says. "He is called Tisquantum."

"What is Patuxet?" one of the townsmen asks.

"This land, these fields and streams, the water washing ashore from the bay is all Patuxet. It was my home, and home to hundreds of others before the sickness came among us," Tisquantum—sometimes called Squanto—says with a sweep of his arm to encompass their view. Grace listens as Squanto tells his tale of kidnapping and transportation to England, where he learned some English words. He ends the story of his long journey home, telling of finding only empty houses and silent cornfields.

"And now your people are here," Squanto states, gesturing to the emerging town. "I come with messages from the great Massasoit, the leader of all the people of this region. He wishes to come to an understanding with your people."

"It will be to our mutual benefit to have good neighbors," one man says.

"Aye, in times of peace and strife, we should look to each other for security."

Grace watches as Squanto and Samoset go to fetch Massasoit. The English men return to their town to prepare for the native leader's arrival. Grace is off on business of her own.

Now that the snow has melted and the spring sun is going to work on the hard ground, Grace starts taking long rambles through the forest of the surrounding countryside. Many days, she can hear the steady chopping as some person or other fells another tree for the continued construction of the town. Sometimes her wandering takes her out of the range of any human sound. It is then that Grace can feel the pull of nature, the bounty of this new land and the desire to find her place in it.

If her time alone in the woods searching for her friend John Goodman has taught her anything, it is that she likes the new freedom this place has to offer. She now knows that she can survive in the wild, and she has friends like John who will look out for her but give her the range to stretch her legs and explore when she wants to. She will always hold a place in her heart for the young pups she left behind in England, but if New England is to be her home, she is content to stay. More than that, she knows she has found her new home.

Returning down the hill from her daylong exploration, she can see all the members of the colony gathered at the bottom of the dirt street gazing out toward the harbor. The *Mayflower* has become a fixture on the harbor scene, like the small islands she was anchored near. Now, as the mastiff follows the gaze of the people below, she sees the *Mayflower* is on the move. Her lower sails are set, and her bow is pointed toward the open sea. On land, some of the people sing quietly, some are praying and all are waving at the ship that has been their

home, their security and their connection with England as it sails away.

Grace thinks of her missed chance to escape to Southampton before they finally departed from Plymouth, England, aboard the old ship. She remembers her friend Will Butten, whom she grew to love during the voyage. She thinks of the months of trials and dangers everyone has faced aboard that ship and afterward. The sun catches the dulled image of the mayflower on the stern as the ship picks up speed from the outgoing tide and the freshening spring breeze. The wind ruffles Grace's fur. She ruffs out a farewell, shakes her great body and heads for the fire she knows will be blazing in the hearth of her new home.

Glossary

BOATSWAIN: Pronounced *bosun*. The crew member responsible for the rigging on a ship and keeping order among the crew.

CAPSTAN: A round vertical winch in the middle of the ship. Sailors push on bars to make it turn when hoisting or lowering heavy weights.

COOK ROOM: The section of the forecastle on a merchant ship where meals are prepared.

CUBBRIDGE-HEAD: A bulkhead on the forecastle and half-deck of a ship.

FORECASTLE: The forward cabin of a ship. The name comes from the time when warships had castle-like structures from which sailors could fight an enemy ship.

FOREMAST: The forward-most mast on a seventeenth-century ship.

GOODMAN: A term of respect and an indication of a middle-class economic station for a man.

GOODWIFE: A term of respect and an indication of a middle-class economic station for a woman.

GREAT CABIN: The best cabin on the ship, reserved for the master of the vessel.

HALF-DECK: The command deck of the ship. It stretches nearly half the overall length of the vessel.

HELMSMAN: A sailor who is responible for steering the ship.

HURDLE: A simple, movable section of fencing often made of woven sticks.

LARBOARD: A common term for the left side of a ship in the seventeenth century.

LEAD LINE: A weighted and marked rope lowered from the side of a ship to estimate the depth of the water.

MASTER (CHRISTOPHER JONES): Refers to a man of high station or economic status. In the seventeenth century, the man who commanded the ship was a master, not a captain.

MERCHANT SHIP: A ship whose primary function is to carry cargo from port to port.

ORLOP DECK: An old term for the lower deck of a ship.

POTTAGE: A dish of boiled grains and vegatables with bits of beef or fish sometimes added. A very common meal for sailors in the seventeenth century was a mess of oats and peas boiled together into a heavy stew.

SHALLOP: A common seventeenth-century multipurpose vessel. The open, double-ended, rowing and sailing boats were often taken on long sea voyages for use near shore. *Mayflower's* shallop was stowed in pieces below deck for the voyage.

SHEETS: Ropes used to pull the lower corners of square sails aft.

SHIP'S BOAT: A rowing boat for a larger vessel. *Mayflower's* ship's boat was probably stowed on the main deck.

STARBOARD: The right-hand side of a ship when looking forward.

WEIGH ANCHOR: To raise the anchor at the start of a voyage.

YARDS: Horizontal timbers suspended off the mast from which the sails are set.

YONKER: A young sailor often sent aloft to set and furl the upper sails.

Author's Note

William Bradford's journal, *Of Plimoth Plantation*, is the source from which we know the most about the famous *Mayflower* voyage. His description of the voyage is only a few paragraphs long, ending with the tantilizing sentence: "But to omit other things (that I may be brief) after long beating at sea they fell with the land which is called Cape Cod." Had Bradford only felt he need not be so brief, we might have more details to work with when re-creating their journey.

Bradford does mention that there were two dogs on board. It is not clear where they came from, who owned them, what happened to them after the ship landed or what their names might have been. I have tried to remain faithful to the historic record, using other sources where Bradford is silent. A ship's master in 1602 brought two mastiffs with him when he explored New England. The dogs' names were recorded as Fool and Gallant. I invented a name for the mastiff on the *Mayflower*. I hope it is one the Pilgrims would have approved of and recognized with connection to their religious beliefs.

Acknowledgements

I want to thank my critique group, who stayed with me on this project since it started out as a simple picture book.

I need to thank and offer my appreciation to my fellow students and the faculty of the Simmons College Graduate Program for Children's Literature. Their insightful comments helped steer this story out of the shoal water I had sailed into early on.

I must thank John Kemp, who has read and made better almost everything I have written in the last twelve years.

Finally, I wish to thank all the staff at Plimoth Plantation, Inc., whom I have been blessed to work with in bringing this story to life for our guests on a daily basis for the past twenty-one years.

—PA

First, I would like to thank Peter Arenstam for writing such a beautiful story and Jeff Saraceno for making this such a wonderful project. I'd like to extend many thanks to the Plimoth Plantation for supplying wonderful reference photos. Now for my models. Thank you to my two sons, Tyler and Todd, who seem to sneak their way into every one of my books, and to my incredibly fun new neighbors who posed for so many pictures. A very special thank-you and hug to a sweet dog named Blade and his gracious parents, Christianne and Robert Walker.

—KBH

About the Author

Peter Arenstam was born on a farm in western Massachusetts but grew up on the coast in historic Plymouth. He first earned his captain's license at the age of eighteen. A graduate of Bates College in Lewiston, Maine, and a professional boat builder, Peter currently works as the manager of the maritime artisans' department of Plimoth Plantation, Inc., where he oversees the repair, restoration and sailing of the reproduction ship *Mayflower II*. His children's books are popular with young readers throughout New England. He is currently enrolled in an MFA program at Simmons College in Boston and still lives with his family on the coast, where this story takes place.

About the Artist

Karen Busch Holman, a BFA graduate of the University of Massachusetts at Amherst, is the illustrator for the Mitt and Minn mouse series, as well as the Nicholas mouse series. Karen's work as an illustrator first appeared in *G Is for Granite, A New Hampshire Alphabet* and its companion book, *Primary Numbers.* She is also the creator of the art that adorns every New Hampshire Heirloom Birth Certificate. Karen's work can be found in numerous publications and books throughout New England. She actively shares her love of art with elementary schools in the Northeast and New England. She recently relocated from East Andover, New Hampshire, to Loveland, Ohio, with her husband, Jeff, and her two sons, Tyler and Todd.